Look out for other books in this series:

Charlie
& The Cat Flap

Charlie
& The Great Escape

Charlie
& The Big Snow

Charlie
& The Rocket Boy

Hilary McKay
Illustrated by Sam Hearn

SCHOLASTIC

To Joseff L Williams
Thank you for all the brilliant letters!
From Hilary McKay

First published in the UK in 2008
by Scholastic Children's Books
An imprint of Scholastic Ltd
Euston House, 24 Eversholt Street
London, NW1 1DB, UK
Registered office: Westfield Road, Southam, Warwickshire, CV47 0RA
SCHOLASTIC and associated logos are trademarks and or
registered trademarks of Scholastic Inc.

ISBN 978 1407 10353 2

British Library Cataloguing-in-Publication Data
A CIP catalogue record for this book is available from the British Library

Typeset by Falcon
Printed by CPI Bookmarque, Croydon
Papers used by Scholastic Children's Books are made
from wood grown in sustainable forests.

1 3 5 7 9 10 8 6 4 2

www.scholastic.co.uk/zone

Best Friends

Charlie and Henry were
best friends. They had
been best friends for
years. They had met
on the Naughty Bench
on their first day at
pre-school when they
were three years old.

Charlie had looked at Henry and thought, I bet I could push him off.

Henry had looked at Charlie and thought, I bet I could squash him flat.

As soon as the three-years-old Charlie and Henry had thought these thoughts, they had tried them out. Sure enough, Charlie had been quite right, he could push

Henry off. And about five seconds later
Henry found that he was also right. He
could squash Charlie flat.

Very soon Charlie and Henry were back on
the Naughty Bench again and for various
reasons they stayed there for the rest of
the morning.

And by home time they were best
friends. Their mothers liked them being

friends. It cheered them up. Secretly
Charlie's mother thought Henry was
slightly worse than Charlie. Secretly
Henry's mother thought Charlie was
slightly worse than Henry. It was nice for
their mothers to think that they had only
the second naughtiest boys in pre-school,
instead of the absolute worst.

Charlie and Henry
lived very close to
each other. They
could play at each
other's houses
whenever they liked,
and when the playing
turned into fighting
they could be marched
home in disgrace with
no trouble at all. Very

soon they were doing almost everything together: Easter egg hunts, haircuts, bonfire night and shoe shopping. Also chicken pox, nits, tummy bugs and colds, because if one of them got something the other one caught it too. One summer they discovered a wasps' nest together and poked it with sticks until they were simultaneously attacked. One winter they both made traps for Father Christmas and very nearly caught him.

When Charlie and Henry started school together their mothers sighed "At last!", hugged each other with relief, and went out to lunch to celebrate. Charlie and Henry spent the next few weeks showing their classmates how easily they could knock each other over, and how well they could squash each other flat. But still, they stayed best friends. During lessons they sat together. At lunch time they ate together. At the end of the day they went home together.

Sometimes teachers got tired of the whisperings and pushings and grabbings that went on at Charlie and Henry's table and tried to separate them. This did not work. Charlie and Henry's behaviour did not change. It just got noisier, because they were further apart.

When Charlie and Henry were seven they moved into Mrs Holiday's class. Mrs Holiday did not try to separate them. She said, "1 might as well keep all the trouble in one place," and gave them a special red table very close to her desk.

"Mrs Holiday colour codes the tables in her room," said Max, Charlie's big brother, who had once been in Mrs Holiday's class himself. "Red for danger."

"Mrs Holiday *likes* us," said Charlie and Henry, but they asked her about their red for danger table, just in case.

"Where ever did you get such an idea?" asked Mrs Holiday.

"Max."

"Goodness!" said Mrs Holiday. "Oh yes, I remember Max! Very tall! School chess team and brilliant at football!"

"What colour was his table?" asked
Charlie.

"I couldn't tell you," said Mrs Holiday.
"He sat right at the back. How would you
two like to be the donkey in our class
Christmas play?"

Charlie and Henry went suddenly silent
with joy and surprise.

"It would be perfect for you!" continued
Mrs Holiday. "Two wonderful starring
parts! The head and the tail. I know I can
trust you not to even think of fighting
about who is which."

Charlie and Henry, who had been about
to fight about that very thing, said that of
course they wouldn't.

"Very well then," said Mrs Holiday, and
so Charlie and Henry, those two best
friends, were the actual donkey in the

actual play and they did it very well.

"Perfect casting," said Mrs Holiday, and
gave them real carrots wrapped in silver
paper for their Christmas presents, instead of
boring chocolate money like everybody else.

"Told you she liked us!" said Charlie to Max.

After the Christmas play it was the end of term.

And then it was Christmas.

And then it was after Christmas, and Charlie and Henry felt like rockets that had gone up into space with a bang and a trail of stars and then come down all grey and flat and dismal to the same old planet Earth.

"Happy New Year! How soon can we take down the decorations?" asked Charlie and Henry's mums.

"Happy New Year! They will soon be back at school," said Charlie and Henry's dads.

"Happy New Year! Cheer up! Only three hundred and fifty eight days till Christmas!" said Max.

None of this cheered Charlie and Henry up at all.

Welcome Back!

Christmas was over. The decorations were down. Now there was nothing to do but wait for Spring, and that was ages away. It was January, the coldest January anybody could remember for years.

Also it was morning on the first day of term, and Mrs Holiday, teacher of Class 3, was in the office meeting a new boy who had just arrived.

Zachary was the new boy. He had arrived very early and all alone. When Mrs Holiday first saw Zachary she thought she had never known a boy so new. He was as new as if he had been plonked down that morning into the middle of an alien world.

Zachary had come with a letter from his last school.

Zachary likes to talk about his family, it said. *But often questions upset him, because he does not know the answers.*

Mrs Holiday could understand that. She did not ask questions. She just smiled and led him along the corridors to her class.

"We have never had a Zachary before," she told him as they walked. "You will be our first."

"Maybe there are no more Zacharys," said Zachary. "Could be that I am the only one."

"That makes us very lucky then, doesn't it?" said Mrs Holiday.

Zachary managed to smile a little.

"Do you know what I say to myself at the start of term?" asked Mrs Holiday. "I say, Courage!"

"Courage?"

"That's right. It helps. And if somebody says it to me, that helps, too!"

"Courage, Mrs Holiday!" said Zachary.

"Courage, Zachary!" said Mrs Holiday, leading him into the empty classroom.

"Now, let me find a home for you!"

She looked around the classroom thoughtfully. Not at the back, where the brainy ones sat, that was too far away. Not with the boys whose favourite thing was football because Zachary from America would not know about English football. Not on the blue table of never-stop-talkers where Zachary would never get a chance to speak. Not on the yellow table of perfect-school-uniform, huge-stuffed-pencil case people either. Zachary had arrived with nothing at all.

"Here you are, Zachary!" she decided at last and pulled out a chair for him. "Quite close to me, and a lovely view of the guinea pig!"

So Zachary sat down and looked quietly at the guinea pig and the guinea pig looked quietly back at Zachary and the room was perfectly silent, waiting for the day to begin.

Meanwhile, Charlie and Henry were on their way to school. Also they were in the middle of a quarrel about Henry's new remote control car (which was lost somewhere at Charlie's house) and Charlie's new electric guitar (which Henry had retuned the day before with terrible string-snapping results).

Charlie and Henry had spent most of the

Christmas holiday quarrelling, starting the day after Christmas when the Curly Wurly from Charlie's Selection Box and the Jelly Santa from Henry's stocking had mysteriously gone missing.

This morning Charlie and Henry were especially grumpy. They had not felt like getting up in the dark and putting on school uniform and eating chilly cereal and plodding up the road in the cold.

WELCOME BACK! read a sign over the school front door.

"I wish I was still in bed!" grumbled Charlie, shrugging off his school bag in the cloakroom and accidentally hitting Henry in the eye.

"*I* wish you were still in bed!" said
Henry crossly, pushing him out of the way.

They stamped into the classroom not
pleased with the world, and there was
Zachary, sitting at their table.

Charlie and Henry were shocked. In an
instant they forgot the Jelly Santa and the
Curly Wurly. The remains of the electric
guitar and the lost remote control car (gone
forever down the back of Charlie's mum's
washing machine) suddenly did not matter.

Instantly they were best friends again, the sort of friends who did not want anybody else. And each of them knew, without saying a word, that of all the people they did not want, they did not want this one most of all. This boy with the round blue eyes and round yellow curls and round pink face and no school uniform.

"Why haven't you got school uniform?" hissed Henry to Zachary, the moment he sat down.

"Because I'm not staying," said Zachary. "I'm only here for a while."

"Just today?" asked Charlie hopefully.

"More than that."

"Just this week then?"

"No, more than that."

"*How* long then?" demanded Charlie, forgetting to whisper, and Mrs Holiday, who had been filling in the register, said, "Charlie!" and glared at him.

Mrs Holiday had a glare like a weapon. Charlie always hated it when she aimed it at him. He could feel exactly where her eyes were pointing. They felt like two icy fingers on the back of his neck. Wriggling made no difference. So Charlie shut up.

"I am trying to fill in the register," said Mrs Holiday, removing the icy fingers from Charlie for a moment and flicking them across to the top of Henry's head. "And I would like a little hush."

Charlie rubbed the back of his neck, and Henry rubbed the top of his head, and they looked across at Zachary to see if he was sorry about getting them into all this trouble. The guinea pig came over to the bars of the cage to look as well. Zachary looked back at all three of them and smiled. A little smile for Charlie and Henry, and then a much bigger one for the guinea pig.

Zachary didn't seem to understand there was any trouble.

He didn't look sorry at all.

Zachary

After she had finished the register Mrs
Holiday introduced Zachary to the class.
She said, "Zachary has come all the way
from America to be with us for a while. I
hope you will all be very good friends.
Would you like to tell us a little bit about
yourself, Zachary?"

For a moment it looked like Zachary

wouldn't. He gazed
around the class as
if there was nothing
he could tell them that
they could possibly
understand. But then he
seemed to change his mind, and he stood up.

He said, "My name is Zachary but most
folks call me Zack. I am seven going on
eight. I have come a long way. My dad is an
astronaut on his way to
a star.

"It will take him two
n'half years to get there,
and two n'half to get back so
I shall be more than thirteen
when I see him again."

Then he sat down.

There was moment of stunned

silence, and then Class 3 erupted. They had never heard such a ridiculous story! They had never heard such awful showing off! Twenty-six hands shot up as high as they could reach. Several people jumped up, so as to get their hands even higher. The noise was immense. It sounded like the classroom was falling apart.

"QUIET, EVERYONE!" said Mrs Holiday in her loudest voice. "HENRY! PICK UP YOUR CHAIR! CHARLIE STOP SHOUTING! HANDS DOWN ALL OF YOU! Now, Zachary!"

"Yes ma'am?" said Zachary politely.

"Thank you for talking to us. It is not easy to stand up like that and talk to so many people. You did very well indeed. Charlie, stop waving your hand about!"

Charlie stopped waving his hand about because Mrs Holiday was looking so fierce. She would not let anyone ask a single question about Zachary's father. She would not let anyone say that what he had told them could not possibly be true. She acted like she believed every word. Only Charlie was allowed to speak, and only after he had promised he really had something sensible to say.

When Charlie was excited or bothered about something his voice went squeaky. It was squeaky now as he said,

"If Zack is seven going on eight and it

takes two'n'half years to get to the star and two'n'half to get back then that is only five years his dad will be gone. So Zack will be twelve when he gets home, not more than thirteen like he said."

"Good Heavens, Charlie!" said Mrs Holiday, looking truly astonished. "I believe that is the first time I have ever heard you do maths on purpose! *And* you got it *right*! Zachary? Please can you explain to Charlie?"

Zachary stood up again, as if he had been asked to explain to the whole class, not just Charlie.

He said, "He's got stuff to do when he gets there. He's not going to go all that way and take all that time and then just turn right round and come back. He's got to look around and do stuff."

Mrs Holiday was giving her class a look which said as plainly as speaking, Move one finger, speak one word, and you are all in at break time!

"He's got seeds to plant," said Zachary.

"*On a star*?!" exploded Henry, before he could stop himself.

"Henry, apologize to Zachary or leave the room!" ordered Mrs Holiday.

"'Pologize, Zachary," muttered Henry furiously.

"Seeds to plant," repeated Zachary, as if nothing at all had happened to interrupt him. "And then, I suppose he'll have to hang around and wait and see if they come up. That'll take time. So, I'm going to be thirteen when he gets back," Zachary paused. "I guess," he said, and sighed.

Mrs Holiday seemed to want to change

the subject. She said it had been very interesting to hear about Zachary's father, and now they would do maths. They were doing charts and graphs, and she said they would make a chart called a bar chart showing everyone's pets. Very quickly she began to write up on the board all the sorts of pets people had. She made everyone help.

They counted five dogs, eleven cats, two rabbits, two hamsters, five guinea pigs, one cockatoo and nineteen goldfish and then Zachary put up his hand and said,

"Four horses."

Charlie and Henry jumped up so fast they banged their heads together.

"Four horses?"

asked Mrs Holiday.

"I have four horses," said Zachary.

Mrs Holiday wrote FOUR HORSES at the bottom of her list on the board and took no notice of Henry and Charlie.

"Anything else?" she asked.

"No, ma'am," said Zachary.

The four horses went on to the chart with all the rest of the animals.

Mrs Holiday would not let anyone say that nobody has four horses.

Once the four horses were down on the list Zachary took no more notice of the maths lesson. He sat through it as if it was something going on far, far away from him. As if he was peacefully watching it through a telescope, slightly interested and slightly sleepy.

It was not the same for the rest of Class

3. To them it seemed the longest lesson
ever, and they themselves felt like balloons
blown up too hard and about to explode.
Even Charlie (newly discovered
mathematical genius) could hardly bear it.

But at last it was break.

The whole class rushed out into the
playground and surrounded Zachary.

They had decided what they thought
about him, with his four horses, and his
dad on a two and a half
year long journey to a
star. They sang,

"Liar, liar! Pants on
fire!

LIAR, LIAR!
PANTS ON FIRE!"

Zachary stood and looked

at them with his hands in his pockets and
a little frown on his forehead, and his
round blue eyes even rounder than ever.

Liar, liar! Pants on Fire!

"Disgraceful!" exclaimed Mrs Holiday, appearing from nowhere and freezing them all into silence with one terrible look.

"Inside, all of you! Zachary, wait here! Charlie and Henry, what do you think you are doing?"

Charlie and Henry had not joined in the singing of "Liar, liar! Pants on fire!" with everyone else. This was because in the mad rush to get out of the classroom Charlie had tripped over his feet and landed sprawled on the ground. While he was rolling around saying, "Oh, oh, nobody cares!" Henry had seen the wonderful chance to sit on his friend's stomach and tie the laces of his two shoes together in a big hard knot.

Charlie and Henry had been too busy huffing and kicking and wrestling to sing. Therefore, when Mrs Holiday stormed outside to her class they escaped the worst of her anger. They were told to stop being silly and put their shoes on properly, and show Zachary around the playground a little and make him feel at home.

Charlie and Henry showed Zachary the football field, the Friendship bench ("You're supposed to sit on it if you haven't any friends," explained Henry, and Zachary obligingly sat down), the old nest that the swallows had built, the outside tap by the caretaker's room, and the teachers' car park.

"Once when it was winter like this, the outside tap dripped," said Charlie, "and

the water made a great puddle in that dip
in the middle of the teachers' car park and
it all froze solid and we made slides. But
they put salt on the slides and fixed the
tap."

Zachary said, "At home there is a whole
lake that freezes solid and we go skating
and sliding in the moonlight and wolves
come out of the trees and sit round the
edge watching, but it's perfectly safe

because they can't run on ice. Having four legs means they slide four ways at once and get nowhere. Of course, they won't come near the bonfires."

Neither Charlie nor Henry had ever been to America, but suddenly they saw in their minds a picture of a frozen lake and moonlight and firelight and shadowy trees and wolves. They saw it so clearly they were stunned, and for ever afterwards, when Charlie and Henry heard the word "America", that was the thing they thought of first. Now they stared at Zachary and their mouths fell open and stayed that way.

That was why they did not say, "Liar, liar! Pants on fire!"

"It is a pity they fixed that dripping tap," continued Zachary, seeming to be talking as much to himself as Charlie and Henry. "I really like skating. Especially at night. On clear frosty nights you can see my father's rocket heading towards his star. I miss my dad. And my mom. She's down in Florida right now. Disneyland."

Just then the bell went and they had to hurry back inside where Mrs Holiday was being so frighteningly polite nobody dared hardly speak for the whole of the rest of the day.

This meant that Henry had no chance of informing Zachary of something he knew for absolutely certain until the end of school.

"Disneyland," said Henry, "is in France! Paris! I've been there! You ask anyone in this class if you don't believe me!"

But Zachary did not ask anyone. He just gazed solemnly at Henry with his round blue eyes, shook his head and said, "I think you are a little mixed up, Charlie."

And then he walked away, leaving Henry to walk home with Charlie chattering with indignation.

"He called me Charlie!" said Henry. "Do I look like you?"

"NO!" said Charlie. "DEFINITELY NOT! You're titchy! You've got weird hair! You've got yoghurt down your front! You wear girls' white socks..."

"You wear a vest," said Henry, which silenced Charlie. "Anyway we're talking about Zachary. Do you know what he said when I told him where Disneyland was? He said I was mixed up! I've *been* there, Charlie!"

"Yes you have," agreed Charlie, adding very quietly to himself, "You showed off about it for weeks."

"I brought you back that giant lolly that pulled your tooth out."

"I know."

MUNCH
CRUNCH

"I don't suppose you've got it any more? Not even the wrapper?"

"Why would I have kept the wrapper?"

"As a souvenir of me going to Disneyland. *Disneyland, Paris*! We could have shown it to Zachary for proof."

"He wouldn't have taken any notice," said Charlie. "He doesn't take any notice of anything, hardly."

Henry admitted that this was true.

"What I think about Zachary," said Henry, "is that saying, 'Liar, liar! Pants on fire!' to him is a complete waste of time."

"What I think about Zachary," said Charlie, "is that listening to him is making my brain feel weird. Like its spinning round and round inside my head."

Henry agreed with that.

"Wolves!" said Charlie.

"I know," said Henry. "Four horses!"

"I know," said Charlie.

"And that rocket! Did you understand any of that?"

"I understood the maths, Henry," said Charlie smugly. "Do you want me to explain?"

"Not right now," said Henry.

Then they plodded on in silence for a while, until Charlie said suddenly, "We didn't say, 'Liar, liar! Pants on fire!'"

"No."

"But it can't be true, all that stuff he told us?"

"No," said Henry. "Of course it can't."

"Why not?"

"Charlie," said Henry impatiently, "Did it *sound* true?"

"No," admitted Charlie. "But..."

"But what?"

"Wouldn't it be good if it was?"

Frost and Ice

Charlie and Henry told their mothers about Zachary.

"Poor little boy!" said Henry's mother.

"Poor!" repeated Henry to Charlie afterwards. "My mum's bonkers! He's got four horses! He's not poor!"

"I should think only millionaires have four horses," agreed Charlie.

"Billionaires!"

"Trillionaires!"

"I've never heard of one of those," said Henry, and Charlie, who was not really sure that he had either, changed the subject by saying, "My mum said to ask him to tea."

"Ask Zachary to tea," said Charlie's mother. "I should like to meet him."

"Why?"

"To be friendly, of course!"

"If I ask him to tea to be friendly, then he will think he is my friend."

"Good."

"I could ask Henry to tea, if you want to have somebody round," suggested Charlie.

"No thank you, Charlie! That is not what I meant."

"I don't see why you wouldn't like to meet Henry just as much as Zachary."

"I have *met* Henry," said Charlie's mother, not very patiently, "I have met him at least once nearly every day for the last four and a half years. I have patched up his knees and got mud out of his hair. I forgave him for trying to drown you that time in the paddling pool. I carted him off to hospital the day he told me he couldn't move his legs for a practice April Fools'. I have cooked him a mountain of dinners and teas and

lunches and suppers. I know him very well
indeed and I WOULD LIKE A CHANGE!"

"Oh."

"So ask Zachary to tea AND THAT'S
AN ORDER!"

"My mum said I've got to ask you to tea,"
said Charlie to Zachary.

"Why?" asked Zachary.

"Because she's bored with Henry."

"*Bored with ME?*" repeated Henry,
amazed and disbelieving. "Was she
joking?"

"No."

"I bet she was," said Henry. "Bored with
me! Ha!"

"She wasn't joking at all," said Charlie.
"She was in a very bad mood. She said she
wanted a change from you and when I

argued she said 'Ask Zachary to tea AND THAT'S AN ORDER!'"

Zachary looked all round the room, at the windows and the doors and the guinea pig cage and under the table. Under the table he seemed to find an answer.

"Anyhow," he said. "I don't like tea."

So that was the end of that.

Over the next few days the frost and ice grew worse. Mrs Holiday began wearing new fur boots for playground duty. "They make her legs look like lovely sheeps' bottoms," remarked one of the girls. Zachary learnt to tell the difference between Henry and Charlie. Nothing else changed.

Zachary's tales grew more and more

unbelievable. He told anyone who would listen about the boiling geysers he had seen ("like mini volcanoes of hot mud," said Zachary), the quad bike he owned back home in America, the tooth he had swallowed during silent reading, and his grandmother in England, who he said was a witch.

Charlie's brain spun round and round

inside his head and he did not know what
to think.

Henry did. Henry had started saying,
"Liar, liar! Pants on fire!" to each new
story, even though he said before that it
was a complete waste of time.

"Somebody has to tell him what we
think," said Henry primly. Charlie said it
as well sometimes, but he did not say it
comfortably because he had actually seen

Zachary swallow the tooth.

The weather continued to be icy cold with bright starry nights. Zachary spent a lot of his break times gazing at the dip in the middle of the teachers' car park, and at the outside tap that did not leak any more. Charlie and Henry used to watch him. They knew he was thinking of his frozen lake where the wolves came out of the trees, and the bonfires burned, and the nights were so clear that you could see a rocket heading for a star two and a half years away.

Then one night Charlie went with his parents to meet his big brother Max from a friend's house. They walked, because Charlie's parents said that would be quicker than defrosting the car. Max's friend lived on the road that went past the school, and on the way home Max and Charlie lagged behind their parents and Charlie told him for the first time the story about Zachary's father and the rocket.

Max looked up at the sky and said, "I wonder which star."

This gave Charlie a creepy feeling down his back, which became ten times more creepy when they passed the school. Because in the shadowy playground he was sure he saw a little figure slip silently round a corner.

There was a sort of glow around the little figure's head, which Charlie guessed was how yellow curls looked by starlight.

"Did you see anyone?" he asked Max.

"Where?"

"In the playground, sort of hiding."

"Mrs Holiday, waiting to pounce?" asked
Max grinning, and did a very good impression
of Mrs Holiday pouncing on Charlie.

"Much smaller than Mrs Holiday," said
Charlie, pushing him away.

"Didn't see anyone," said Max, "but we
can go back and look if you like."

"No!" exclaimed Charlie in sudden alarm, and to prevent Max doing such a thing added, "Race you to Mum and Dad!" and skidded away up the road before Max could disagree.

Max tore after him, and between them they nearly swept their mother off her feet, and then they ran on down the road together, dodging the shadows under the darkest hedges, leaping the blackness of silent open gates, collapsing with thumping hearts at each friendly lamp post.

The more they ran, the better Charlie felt. It was delicious to be frightened and running in the night if you had your big brother beside you, your mum and dad not far behind, and home just round the corner with the lights on and Suzy the cat watching out from the windowsill. He forgot the little figure that he had half seen in the playground.

But when the house was quiet and he was safe in bed for the night he remembered and, despite his quilt, and his extra fleecy blanket, and his dinosaur hot water bottle and his winter pyjamas, the memory made him shiver.

Had that been Zachary in the playground?

He wished now that he and Max had gone back to see.

But we didn't, thought Charlie. We ran home.

Then he remembered Zachary saying, that first unfriendly day, "I have come a long way."

You cannot run home to America, thought Charlie. You cannot run home to a star.

Poor Zachary, thought Charlie.

It was the first time ever he had thought that thought.

Terrible Trouble

The next day there was terrible trouble at school. Overnight, the car park had become a black sheet of ice. The Head Teacher's car skidded and smashed into the caretaker's room with a horrible scrunching sound. The caretaker had rushed outside to see what was happening and had fallen and broken his leg. Then an ambulance arrived and drove the caretaker to hospital, and after that a breakdown truck came to school and took the Head Teacher's car away.

Mrs Holiday also had trouble on the car park ice. She slipped down so hard in her sheeps' bottom boots that she had a great black bruise all up one arm, and another on the side of her head that made one eye swell up. But she would not allow herself

to be taken away like the caretaker and the Head Teacher's car. She came into class and she said, "The school car park is totally out of bounds. That outside tap leaked so much that the whole area is one huge patch of ice. Poor Mrs Smith's car is wrecked and later on we will all make Get Well Cards for the caretaker, who has broken his leg."

Then she shot icy cold glares all around the room from her one good eye.

Charlie felt sick. He thought he was going to have to tell on Zachary, and he did not want to. He thought of himself and Max racing past to their parents and their warm safe home, and he remembered the loneliness he had glimpsed in the playground the night before. He did not understand Zachary any more than he had the first day they met, but suddenly he was on his side, and he did not know what to do.

Zachary knew what to do.

Zachary stood up and said, "It was me. I am very sorry. I turned on the tap last night. I wanted to make a frozen lake."

Mrs Holiday looked at Zachary as if she loved him and she said, "That was a very brave and honest thing to say, Zachary. Very brave and very honest. I am proud of you."

Then Henry was so ashamed that he had ever sung "Liar, liar! Pants on fire!" to Zachary that he put his head down on the table and started to cry.

Nobody else said a word, not even Mrs Holiday, until Charlie called out, in his squeakiest voice, "I am proud of him too!"

and he put one arm round Henry, and the
other round Zachary.

"I wish he was stopping for always, not
just for a while," said Charlie.

The Rocket and the Star

Charlie's wish did not come true. Just
when they got used to him, Zachary said,
"I've got to go."

"WHAT?!" shouted Charlie and Henry.

If Charlie and Henry were shocked
when Zachary came they were absolutely
outraged when he said he had to go.

"You can't!" they said. "You've only just

got here! Who says you've got to? What do you mean, go?"

"Back," explained Zachary.

"Back where?"

"Just back," said Zachary, who never seemed to know where he was, except that it was not home. "Soon."

"Soon?" asked Charlie. "When is soon?"

"Saturday."

"*Saturday! It's Tuesday now!*"

"We've hardly got to know him!" complained Charlie to Max.

"You didn't want to know him."

"He never even came to tea."

"Whose fault was that?"

"There's loads he never told us!"

"Would you have believed him if he had?" Recently Max had somehow heard about the singing, "Liar, liar! Pants on

Fire!" He had told Charlie what he thought of that.

"But there isn't time for anything!" Charlie complained.

"There was time," said unsympathetic Max. "You were horrible, all of you! A gang of little rotters, thinking you knew everything! You don't look further than the ends of your stuck up noses!"

"Neither do you," growled Charlie, but really he knew that it was not true. Max had not said "Liar!" Max had said, "I wonder which star."

"What can I do?" wailed Charlie. "How can we make it up?"

"Think," said Max.

Charlie thought. He chewed his knuckles and thought. He pulled his hair and

thought. He pounded his head into his pillow and thought and thought and at last he had an idea.

"But it might not be a good one," he said to Henry. "How can I tell?"

"Ask Mrs Holiday," said Henry.

"It might be good," said Mrs Holiday, when she heard it. "Let me talk to Zachary."

"Yes."

"And his grandmother."

"All right."

"And check the weather forecast."

"I forgot about that."

"And we'd have to send letters home."

"All those things," said Charlie, and sighed.

"I will do them as fast as I can," said Mrs Holiday, but all the same it was Thursday before she could tell him, "It was a good idea!"

On Friday afternoon Mrs Holiday's class stayed on after school. They had biscuits and blackcurrant juice and a chocolate cake delivered by Zachary's grandmother (who said very little and went away early and certainly looked like a witch). After

that they played
games until the
windows grew
black and outside
it was proper
dark night.

Then at last
Mrs Holiday said it was time to get ready
and they all wrapped up warm and went
out into the playground, and Zachary
pointed to where they should look.

Everyone saw quite plainly the rocket and
the star.

ONE

It was lunch time at school and Charlie and Henry were sitting together. They always sat together because they were best friends. Charlie and Henry had been best friends for five years, ever since they met on the Naughty Bench at Pre-school. They

Nobody understood Henry as well as Charlie did, and nobody understood

Charlie as well as Henry did. So when Charlie said to Henry, "You can have my cheese and onion crisps if you want! They give you such a ponky smell!"

Henry understood at once.

"You don't usually mind smelling ponky." he said. "Usually you like them the best! You've gone bonkers again, haven't you?"

Charlie smiled and did not say he hadn't.

"Who is it this time?" demanded Henry. "No, don't tell me! I can guess! It's the new student teacher that came this morning!"

Charlie's smile got worse than ever, and he gazed across the dining hall at the new student teacher.

"What's her name?" asked Henry. "I

wasn't listening when she said."

Charlie shrugged. He hadn't been listening either. He didn't think her name mattered. She was simply the New Miss, fascinating and lovely because she had long red curly hair and a leather thong round her neck with a stone threaded on to it.

"I can't see anything special about her," said Henry, "She gets ratty dead easy and she looks like a witch. That stone round her neck is just a normal boring stone."

"I know. I heard her tell Lulu she found it on the beach."

"That's not a good reason to wear it round her neck," said Henry. "I found a dead seal on the beach once..."

"You've told me a million times!"

"...A *huge* dead seal..."

"Seals aren't that huge," objected Charlie.

"They look much bigger dead than they do in zoos. Parts of it had been chewed or something. It smelled a bit like..." (Henry glanced into Charlie's lunch box) "...ham sandwiches and a bit like it had died of old age..."

"I don't know why you're telling me all this *again*!" groaned Charlie.

"I'm just explaining that it definitely wasn't the sort of thing you'd want to wear round your neck..."

Charlie picked the ham out of his sandwich and pushed it down Henry's collar. A dinner lady caught him ham-handed and sent him to stand by the wall. Henry trailed after him because they were friends and they continued gazing at the

New Miss.

"Rubbish shoes," remarked Henry.

"Girls," said Charlie, "only ever look good in very high heels or roller skates. I don't see why they don't just wear them all the time. I would."

"You'd fall over all the time then."

"I wouldn't," said Charlie, rolling his eyes at Henry's silliness, "because I'd be a *girl*! Dope!"

Henry fished a bit of ham up from under his collar and ate it. He did not bother to argue any more. He knew it would be no good. Falling in love did weird things to Charlie's brain. Now (like countless times before) he would give up cheese and onion crisps, try and teach himself football tricks, spend a great deal of time smiling and leaning against walls, and arrange his hair in unnatural formations of swirls and spikes with hair gel borrowed from Henry's vast hair gel collection.

There was only one good thing about Charlie in love.

"It never lasts long," said Henry thankfully.

Lunch ended, Henry and Charlie went outside and the New Miss went back to the classroom. Charlie practised football tricks as close to the window as he dared while Henry kept an eye on her through the glass and from time to time said helpfully, "She's not watching... Good job she didn't see that... she's still not watching...."
The New Miss did not survive the afternoon. First she ruined Art by handing

out paper plates and demanding they all draw healthy salads and then she gave out worksheets about Henry the Eighth with pictures of all of his six unfortunate wives.

"Label the wives and colour them in," she ordered.

Charlie gave all six red floppy hair and stones round their necks and the New Miss put his worksheet in the recycling bin.

"I hope you are not trying to be rude," she said.

Charlie, who could be much ruder than that without trying at all, was very offended indeed.

Henry was right; he decided, she did look like a witch.

Meet Charlie - he's trouble!

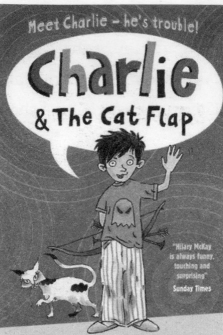

Charlie and Henry are staying the
night at Charlie's house. They've made
a deal, but the night doesn't go quite
as Charlie plans. . .

Meet Charlie - he's trouble!

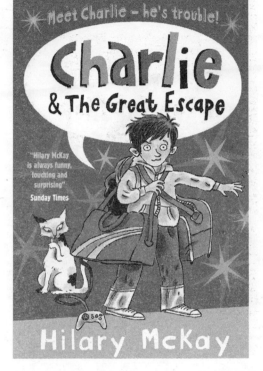

Charlie's fed up with his mean family always picking on him – so he's decided to run away. That'll show them! Now they'll be sorry!

But running away means being boringly, IMPOSSIBLY quiet…

Meet Charlie – he's trouble!

"The snow's all getting wasted! What'll we do? It will never last till after school!"

Charlie's been waiting for snow his whole life, but now it's come, everyone's trying to spoil it! Luckily, Charlie has a very clever plan to keep it safe…